AF191322

Previously published by TWINS as a print book and e-book in the Black Tiger series:

Book 1 Coming Home
  Volume 1 Arrival
  Volume 2 Marcello

TWINS

1 Coming Home
Volume 2 Marcello
Black Tiger book series

Novel

From the German

by TWINS

English first edition

Bibliographic information of the German National
Library: The German National Library lists this
publication in the German National Bibliography;
detailed bibliographic data is available on the Internet at
http://dnb.dnb.de.

Title of the original German edition: Schwarzer Tiger 1
Coming Home: Band 2 Marcello © 2023 TWINS by BoD
- Books on Demand, Norderstedt

© 2024 English first edition and translation: TWINS

Cover design and illustrations: TWINS

Editing and proofreading: TWINS

Set: TWINS

Production and publisher: BoD - Books on Demand,
Norderstedt

ISBN 978-3-7578-1566-0

 www.schwarzertiger.com

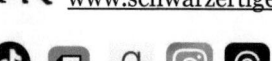

TwinsSchwarzerTiger

Then a movement, a small animal scurried across the path in front of us.

"What was that?" I asked.

"A little wandering mouse."

"What animals are you hunting?" We set off again.

"Everything, but mainly large animals. There's a forest not far from here. I usually hunt there."

"How often do you do that?"

"Every three days."

"And do you sell the meat?"

"No. I eat this on my own. Straight after hunting in the forest."

"Oh, so you'll grill it right there? I didn't know you were allowed to do that."

"I don't grill it."

I stopped and let go of him. "Then how do you eat it?" I stared at him.

Marcello glared at me, his eyes sparkling in the darkness. "Well, like this."

"Raw?" I exclaimed in horror and he nodded. "But that's not possible!"

"My stomach can handle it. It's different to your stomachs. My father did it the same way."

"Okay." I kept walking, was there really such a thing? Special people who ate raw meat? So, he sat in the forest and cut pieces of meat out of the animal, which he immediately ate with all the blood on it! I shook myself! And I had thought he was a vegetarian! No wonder the others at the table had laughed at me! He tried to put his arm around me again, but I shook him off.

"What is it?" he asked.

"That's why Gregory calls you Tiger! Because you eat like a tiger!"

He shook his head. "No, he calls me that because I'm a tiger." Another piece of nonsense.

"Yes, he said the same thing when I asked him. What do you mean, you're a tiger?"

He stopped, I stopped too and looked at him curiously. Suddenly his outline blurred and a black tiger stood in front of me! Then everything blurred again and he stood there again. "Do you understand now?" What had just happened? Had I just seen a black tiger? "I am a tiger," he said calmly.

I shook my head. Okay, I was dreaming. The date with him was still pending; I had fallen asleep and dreamed everything. Or I was still lying on the bed. There was a thunderstorm outside and of course, he had left and what a pity, we hadn't kissed after all. Too bad, but what a lovely dream!

"Everything okay?" he asked.

"Yes, this is a dream. You're not real and I'll probably wake up soon, because that's always the case when you realize you're dreaming."

"This is not a dream."

"Yes, yes, says the dream Marcello!" I glanced around. It was really impressive what the human mind could come up with! I could have bet that it was all real.

"Kathleen, don't be afraid."

"I'm not! It's a funny dream, can we fly too? I love flying in dreams! C'mon, let's try it!"

He laughed. "I can't fly. Shall we keep walking?" Somehow the flying thing didn't work out, never mind. Funny that I hadn't woken up yet.

We walked on and I hung on to him. "Tell me about yourself, how did you become a tiger?" I mumbled sleepily.

I felt him shrug his shoulders. "I was born like this and have been a tiger since I was a child. My father was a tiger too. And my children might become tigers too. It's in our genes, my father always said."

"Aha. In the genes. Very funny!" What an extraordinary dream fantasy I had, awesome! "And isn't anyone afraid of you?"

"Why would they?"

"Because tigers attack and kill people!" Hopefully I'd remember the dream a bit, then I'd tell him tomorrow and he'd have a laugh about it. Although, he'd probably be mad at me for leaving him out in the rain; so, I'd just tell Debbie and Claudia.

"Neither my father nor I have ever attacked people! I hunt for my food in the forest and it's all animals."

"And why are you walking around as a human if you're a tiger?"

"Because it's easier. But my true form is the tiger. I also work as a tiger in the shaft and I am a tiger when I'm alone. Only in company do I adapt." Interesting, now my subconscious had even processed the horror when I had discovered the screen in the tunnel and thought I was seeing an animal there.

"And why?"

"Why what?"

"Why are you blending in? Does someone have something against your true form? Or doesn't everyone know?"

"Everyone knows it. Nobody has anything against it. It's just easier. As a tiger, I can't sit on a chair at the table. I can also talk better as a human."

"You can talk as a tiger?" I laughed; I hadn't dreamt anything so silly and stupid in a long time!

"Yes, but it's more telepathic. You'll then hear my voice in your head." This just got better and better! "We're back."

I glanced up, that's right! We were standing in front of Claudia's house again. "It's incredible how realistic this all looks for a dream!" He fell silent and I regarded him. "What's wrong?"

"Kathleen, I'm sorry," he sounded worried, "but this is reality. You're really not dreaming!"

"Yes, yes!" I yawned; I was tired. He took me in his arms and covered my face with kisses; I smiled. Please don't wake up now, please! I loved dreams like that!

"See you at the movies tomorrow?" he whispered and I nodded. Cool, my subconscious had even memorized that! "Good night, city girl!"

"Female miner!" I objected.

"Okay, female miner!" He grinned; I could hear it in his voice.

"See you tomorrow, Marcello!" We kissed and I wished it was real. But it was all just too good to be true. Then he was gone and I stepped into the house through the patio door, which was still open. So now I would go to bed in my dream. How absurd, but I did and fell asleep.

Bright sunlight woke me up! I smelled coffee and opened my eyes, where was I? Oh yes, with Claudia! Why was I wearing my clothes? Then I remembered that crazy dream from last night with Marcello and that he was supposed to be a tiger! I laughed, pure madness! I remembered everything and it was so crystal clear, amazing! Then it was no wonder that I still had my clothes on; I really had fallen asleep listening to music. It was just funny that the cell phone was on the bedside table; I must have put it there in my sleep. Next time I should put my dirty dishes next to the bed. Maybe I would wash them while I was sleeping and grinned. That would be some-thing, a useful sleepwalker! I wonder if there was anyone like that? I'd hire him right away! Doubly effective! He would clean and tidy my house day and night. I lolled on the bed, that had been a wonderful dream! I hadn't flown, but Marcello and I had kissed the whole time, that was so lovely! And then the romantic walk through the forest at night, maybe I continued dreaming tonight?

The smell of coffee hit my nose again, now I realized - Claudia must be back! I immediately jumped up, I was already dressed, and ran down to the kitchen, and right! "Claudia!"

"Kathleen!" We fell into each other's arms. "I hope I didn't wake you up?"

I shook my head. "No worries! How are you? How's your father-in-law? How was your trip? Oh, you wouldn't believe how happy and delighted I am to see you!"

"Yes, I'm very happy too!" We had now greeted each other enough and let go of one another. "The journey was good and we're all doing well under the circumstances. I'm tired but glad to be back. Dirk has stayed with his father and his condition is stable. He's going to stay there for a while, also to support his mother; she's still pretty down with nerves."

"Oh dear, the poor thing," I sighed sympathetically and stroked Claudia's back. "I hope he gets better soon."

"I hope so, too. Now tell me, I heard you were at the mountain with Uncle Ben?"

"At the mountain?" I laughed. " I wished! I was IN the mountain!"

"Not really?"

"Yes, deep down in the tunnel!"

"What? I wasn't even there yet!"

"Really?"

She laughed. "Well, you've really impressed the men with yourself, haven't you?"

"Mind you! I'm one of them now, they said! I've been in the Father's with several miners!"

"Oh, the shabby pub!"

"They have good food!"

"Pretty meaty, you know Dirk is a vegetarian. So, we never eat there and our close friends don't necessarily hang out there either," she grinned. I understood what she meant. I'd given Gregory a similar answer yesterday when he'd asked me what I did with my friends in the city. But this wasn't the city and it had been really cozy with the men there. And Moni had already become really likeable to me in the short time with her warm manner. I also had the feeling that I belonged, as if I was part of a team. I didn't have that feeling at work and even with my friends it was as if we were together and yet everyone was on their own. Not so yesterday in the pub. Everyone somehow stuck together, but of course only if you were part of it!

"Debbie came in and was totally bullied!" I said gloomily.

"Yes, her fiancé is in prison," she nodded.

"So what? That's no reason to bully someone!" I got upset.

"It's a small village, people talk. That's the way it is here. I try to stay out of the village gossip and remain neutral."

That sounded very sensible, but I wasn't like that - I was far too curious for that. "Then you haven't heard of section B either?"

"Section B? Isn't that where Marcello's father had an accident?"

"Exactly! Speaking of Marcello, what do you think of him?"

"Did you meet him, yes?" she smiled.

I nodded; I could come back to the details later. "And what do you think of him?"

"He's a handsome one! And quite hard-working! Do you like him?" she continued smiling.

"Yes, but I really scared him off yesterday. We had actually arranged to go for a walk."

"Oho! So?"

"I canceled."

"Why?"

"Because I don't want an affair. I want a relationship." She nodded sympathetically. "It's obvious that there's not much of a future with a miner from here," I added.

"Don't say that!" she teased me. "Later you'll find the love of your life and move here! Dirk and I would be very happy!"

"And Debbie too!" I added. "Do you do a lot with her?"

She shook her head. "Since the thing with her fiancé, she keeps to herself a lot. We see each other when we go shopping and exchange a few words, but apart from that we don't talk much."

"But you're neighbors!"

She nodded. "I don't have that many close friends here in the village, most of them are quite simple-minded. My friends live in the larger neighboring village, where Dirk also works."

"Marcello is not a simple person," I replied. She certainly didn't mean it that way, but somehow the description of the villagers sounded derogatory to me. I wonder if she would describe her uncle in the same way? Probably, although I had thought something similar.

"He's very intelligent, he could easily have gone to university!" she agreed.

"I think so too! Why didn't he?"

She shrugged her shoulders. "I think he wanted to stay here with his family and friends in his village. He would have had to move to the city to study. Most people stay here and the only job opportunities here are in mining."

"Hm, that's right. I really have to tell you about my super funny dream, it was really intense! I dreamt that I was going for a walk with him and we were kissing. Suddenly he turned into a black tiger and said it was his true form! Crazy, isn't it?" I laughed, such nonsense, but she remained serious. "Isn't that hilarious?" I chuckled.

"You do realize he's really a tiger, right?"

"Yeah, sure!" I laughed even louder, she messed with me and waited for her to laugh along, but she didn't.

"Kathleen, you know he's a tiger?"

"What's this nonsense, Claudia? I'm not falling for your joke! Don't you think it's funny?"

"I don't know if you really kissed him or dreamed that part, but he really is a tiger. This part wasn't a dream."

I stopped laughing. "You're seriously telling me he's a tiger?"

"Yes." She still remained serious.

"So?" I waited for the punch line.

"I was also surprised at first when I moved here. He was like that as a child and his father was also a tiger, so everyone was used to it. Of course, I found it unusual at first, but now it's nothing special for me anymore."

I felt dizzy! Either I was dreaming again or this and yesterday were reality! I ran into the bathroom, splashed ice-cold water on my face - I was clearly awake. If that was the case, it meant we really had kissed! I had let him into the kitchen and we had gone for a walk, was that possible? Wasn't there any proof that I hadn't actually been dreaming? The towel!

"Kathleen, are you OK?" she asked, standing anxiously in the doorway.

I opened the laundry container, it was empty! I breathed a sigh of relief. So, he hadn't been here, because he had put it inside there! Then maybe it was a dream after all?

"Are you looking for that?" She pointed to a gray towel. Ice-cold shivers ran down my spine as I stared at it, stunned! "It was damp, that's how I hung it up. Otherwise, it would get moldy in the laundry container."

That was the proof! I threw my hands up to my face in shock, my knees went weak and I sank to the floor. "Oh Claudia, I didn't dream that! We really did kiss!" I stammered in horror; she smiled.

"And would that be so bad?"

Pale, I glanced up at her, still squatting next to the container. "It is, if he's a tiger! I don't want to be with a freak! He eats raw meat!"

"He's not a freak!"

"Oh, no? So, you think he's normal?

"Who is normal? Are we normal? Are you normal?"

"After all, I'm a human being! I think that's relatively normal!" I objected.

"Don't be so petty. Now you've met a man and you've even kissed him and you have found something wrong with him again. I've told you before, there's no such thing as Mr. Perfect. You have to make compromises in every relationship. You didn't like your last boyfriend because he was a smoker; the one before that because he was too old and now Marcello because he's a tiger. So really, you'll never be able to find anyone like this, Kathleen!"

"But I think there's a world of difference between being a smoker and being a tiger!"

"Even if so, you didn't like the smoker and Marcello doesn't smoke and is a really handsome boy. All the girls are crazy about him."

"Then why is he single?"

She was silent for a moment. "He had a girlfriend, unfortunately she died."

"Did he mangle her in her sleep?" I asked sarcastically.

She glared at me angrily, which was rare for her. "No! She died in the shaft!"

"In the shaft?"

"Section B."

"Section B!" I exclaimed in horror and she nodded.

"He was almost involved in the accident when he tried to save his father. She sort of died in his place when she saved him."

"But if he hadn't tried to save his father, she wouldn't have had to save him and they would both still be alive!"

She sighed sadly. "He would definitely have tried. If it hadn't been for her, he would be dead now." We were both silent. That shed a whole new light on him, how tragic! His girlfriend had given her life for his, how terrible! How had he been able to cope with the death of two loved ones and still retain his joy of life? I thought back to our conversation in the kitchen yesterday, where he said that he was a serious man. I believed that one hundred percent! "C'mon, let's have a coffee," she said conciliatory and offered me her hand.

I grabbed it and she pulled me to my feet. "I can really use that now!" I smiled gratefully at her. We talked about this and that. Dirk's work, the work on the house; their planned vacations, past vacations. "What is our schedule for today? I have it from a reliable source that you're going to the outdoor movies with your cinema group tonight?" I grinned. "And if yesterday wasn't a dream, then I've already promised Marcello that I'll go with him and Gregory inexplicably assumes that I accompany him too," I added sorrowfully.

Amused, she laughed and was apparently no longer angry with me, thankfully. "I can see that I won't be able to sit next to you when you're surrounded by handsome men on both sides."

"Don't tell me you think Gregory is handsome!" I asked skeptically.

"At least he's not a tiger! You see, you don't have to choose Marcello," she teased me.

"Then rather a tiger than Gregory!"

"Poor Gregory! He's otherwise very, very popular with the girls!"

"Even more than Marcello?"

She nodded. "He's sort of the leader, if you can call it that, of their clique of friends. And because he's so eloquent and informed, he gets all the girls."

"You probably mean big-mouthed and know-it-all!"

She laughed again. "Oh dear, oh dear! A girl who doesn't fancy him. You do realize, Kathleen, that this makes you even more attractive to him? He'll do everything he can to win you over!"

"I'm not going to be the only girl who doesn't fancy him!"

She shook her head. "But almost the only girl he hasn't had anything with yet!"

"What, really? Unbelievable!" Okay, he was tall, slim; blond, blue-eyed; just the nice guy next door. And that's exactly what I didn't like about him. He was just too smooth without any real edges and corners, whereas Marcello was simply unique! It occurred to me that if Gregory really did get all the girls first, maybe that was why Marcello had rushed our date? Maybe he didn't want to risk losing me to him, could that be? But would he really trust me to fall for this guy? Although Gregory had somehow managed to arrange a movie date with me today anyway. But as I'd decided to take Debbie with me, I was sure I'd be able to keep him at a distance. He didn't seem to like her very much; she'd probably turned him down! I grinned at the idea; his ego certainly hadn't taken it well. "Have you had anything going on with him?" I asked curiously. She laughed and shook her head in the negative. "C'mon," I teased her, "I won't tell Dirk about it either!"

"I was only just able to hold myself back!" she giggled.

"Honestly, I'm relieved!"

At that moment, her phone rang. "That must be him!" she exclaimed delightedly, but her face darkened during the conversation. She hung up and sighed.

"Bad news?" My heart was pounding, what now?

She nodded. "Yes, unfortunately, his father is getting worse again. Dirk will definitely be staying there longer."

"Oh, I'm so sorry about that," I murmured sadly. And what about you? I wanted to scream, are you going there again? Are you going to leave me here alone again? Or would it be better if I left?

She seemed to read my thoughts and smiled at me. "But that doesn't stop you enjoying your vacation with us! And yes, we're going to the movies tonight and tomorrow is a very special event."

"The infamous beach party!" I exclaimed with relief; a weight lifted from my shoulders. I really hoped he would get better soon! But what if his condition continued to deteriorate and she drove back? Well, then I would go home! But somehow, I was beginning to like it here. It was like everyone said, you just couldn't spend your vacation at home. The few days on site had relaxed me more than two weeks of vacation there. Maybe because I was distracted here and nothing reminded me of my worries and problems from home.

"I see you're well informed, and the summer party really is a highlight! I'm sure you'll love it. It takes place down at the beach in the beach bar. Everything will be decorated with lights, garlands and lanterns. There will be fantastic cocktails and, of course, a night-time view overlooking the ocean."

"Sounds good!" Ocean view, beach, there was nothing like this in the city. Sure, there was heaped-up sand and large lakes, but no sea.

"And it really is very romantic there. It has a small dance floor with wooden planks on the ground, surrounded by fairy lights and animated by couples dancing closely together, such as Kathleen with Marcello ..."

"Hey, don't say that!" I laughed, embarrassed.

"He'll definitely be there! The whole village will be there! Young, old; us, you and ..."

"Gregory!" I interrupted her.

"Of course, him too! I'm starting to think you do like him!"

"Claudia, how dare you!" I shouted indignantly. "One more insult like that and I'll leave immediately!"

Now she laughed for the first time since Dirk's call, although her eyes remained serious. "You'll be raving about this evening to your city girls in a year's time, I'm telling you! So now we should get going and buy some food. This is a village; all the stores are closed at the weekend."

"All right! Shall I help with the dishes?"

"Kathleen, this is not a single household. Of course, we have a dishwasher!"

"All the more reason to want a partner by your side," I grumbled.

"Get ready in peace. I'll tidy up a bit here and then we'll go."

In the guest room I grabbed my cell phone and took a glance at it on the way to the bathroom, aha! I had received a message! I skillfully opened it with one hand, from Paula! "How was it with your tiger yesterday?"

I grinned, that was typical, she couldn't wait to hear the news! My grin disappeared. In the bathroom I took off my clothes and thought about how I should describe last night to her. She would never believe me! I couldn't believe it myself! But since she had already asked, I could answer truthfully. So, I wrote, "He really is a tiger. We kissed. It was great! We're seeing each other tonight for the outdoor movies." I got in the shower and thought about him. About his kisses, his hugs; his firm, slim yet muscular body. His eyes, loving yet with that certain cheeky gleam in them, tiger eyes!

Later in the car, on the way to the shops, I was still thinking about them. "You know, Claudia, not all men can look like that."

"Look how?" She was focused on the road.

"How should I describe it - wild, a little danger-ous, reckless, full of passion and yet loving and tender!"

She laughed with amusement. "Are you thinking of someone in particular?"

"Me? No! Why would you think that?" But I was grinning too. Somehow, I was looking forward to seeing him, my stomach was tingling. I was actu-ally very happy! Was he feeling the same? My gaze wandered to the mountain where he was now working, as he had said, in his true form.

The true figure.

I imagined him as a black tiger, just as I had seen him briefly yesterday, unbelievable!

We stopped in front of a small store. "We're here, in the local shopping center." Her voice dripped with irony; I grinned. "You can get the essentials here. Everything else is available in the larger neighboring village."

Inside, it really did look very tranquil. At least we found what we were searching for straight away and didn't have to think long about what to take, as there was no choice. At the checkout, the saleswoman gave us a friendly smile. "Claudia and Kathaleena, how nice of you to visit me."

Claudia suppressed a grin. "Kathaleena?" she whispered amusedly under the loud clatter of the cash register.

"Yes, nice, isn't it? Thanks to your uncle," I whispered back. The saleslady had put on a thick pair of reading glasses and was laboriously typing in each amount. The ribbons on her glasses dangled left and right from her temples in flashy green. With a loud bang and ringing, the cash drawer popped open; I flinched in shock.

Claudia laughed. "Not used to old cash registers anymore, are you? They still make noise."

"Ah, Kathaleena, I've got something else for you," said the shop assistant, her eyes appearing huge through her glasses.

"For me?" Flabbergasted, I accepted the brown paper bag she handed me. Who could put something back for me? Perhaps a gift from Marcello? A small token of kindness? I peeked inside eagerly, it smelled musty. Disgusted, I kept my distance and opened it more. "My shoes!" I exclaimed in surprise and pulled them out. "The heel is back on? How is that?"

She smiled. "Ben gave them to Wil, who passed them on to my husband. You must know he's a cobbler."

"He also makes shoes," Claudia let me know.

"Great, thank you! How much does that make?"

The sales clerk shook her head. "Ben still owed us one anyway."

"Yes but," I stuttered, "I can really pay for it."

"Thank you very much! See you soon and best wishes to your husband!" Claudia pushed me out, shaking her head outside. "Kathleen, you mustn't be unkind here."

"Where was I unkind?"

"Didn't you realize how you'd offended her by trying to pay with your stubbornness? She already told you everything was fine."

"Yes, but I'm here for a visit and your uncle already paid for my meal yesterday, although it was more his mining buddy. Whatever, he certainly doesn't have to pay for my shoes! It's really nice of him to have them repaired for me anyway."

"Exactly! Tell him thank you and as I understand it, he didn't pay anything because he still owed them. And then you just say thanks to her, and don't waste too many words. Otherwise, you'll offend people, okay?"

"Hm ... okay." I still hadn't quite understood, but I had my shoes back!

"That was Gregory's mom, by the way."

"Oh yeah?"

"You'll see how small the world is here."

"I can already tell!" Back in the car I regarded the high heels, terrific! Really great! I would have thrown them away, when had he given them to Wil? Maybe when we went out to eat? In any case, I hadn't noticed.

Claudia and I cooked together at home. "When does the movie start?" I asked.

"Half past nine." A shudder ran through me, soon I would see Marcello again!

It took me longer to get dressed today than yesterday. It was warm outside. The sun was still shining and the shoes had been repaired. So, I had more options and decided to wear them again straight away. I could now combine them with the blue strap dress with the white flowers. They were only embroidered in a small way and lined the collar and the bottom of the dress, inconspicuous and yet effective. I regarded myself in the mirror and resembled the female version of Gregory. Blue eyes, blonde hair; no rough edges, just the nice girl next door. Maybe that's why I didn't like him. Together we would look like a page out of a reading book. Gregory and Kathleen were good friends and played ball with each other every day, my reflection grimaced. In contrast, when Marcello stood next to me with his dark skin, brown eyes and black hair ... Now my reflection beamed enraptured and my cheeks turned rosy. Oh dear, did I really look that in love when I thought about him? I quickly glanced away. The outfit was finished and today I put on my make-up and didn't wipe it off again.

At some point, Claudia called for me, my heart leapt with excitement and I finished my eyeliner. "I'm coming!" I shouted, grabbed my handbag, threw my cell phone in, I had money too - I was ready to go!

"Wow! Well, if someone hasn't made themselves up!" Her gaze wandered down my body and back up again.

"Oh, maybe a little!" I smiled sheepishly.

"By the way," she said as I carefully descended the steps in my high heels, "Marcello left his shoes here yesterday."

I peeked around the corner in amazement. There were the mining boots, I had completely forgotten about them! "No, they're mine," I mumbled glumly and she laughed at me. "Don't ask, let's go!"

Outside, I remembered in a flash that I had completely forgotten about Debbie! We hadn't arranged to meet at some point, but we still wanted to stay in touch. "Claudia! I'm just going to run over to Debbie's! We can take her with us, can't we?" She raised her eyebrows questioningly, but I didn't wait for her answer and stalked over to Debbie's house.

This time Debbie opened the door and beamed at me. "Oh, Kathleen! You look so pretty!"

"Thank you! It's cinema today! We wanted to pick you up!"

Her smile disappeared. "Oh, I'm staying at home tonight."

"Why? The great, super outdoor movie night is just waiting for you! Besides, you have to protect me from Gregory! I think he's trying to pick me up!" I grimaced and only now realized that she had frozen.

"No, thanks." With that she closed the door in my face, what was the matter with her? Had I said something wrong?

Confused, I went to the street where Claudia was waiting with the engine running and got in.

"And?" she asked.

"You can drive off, she's not coming," I muttered disappointedly and she stepped on the gas.

"It's not up to you. I've already told you that she prefers to stay at home and not go out much," she comforted me.

"She was at the Father's yesterday to talk to Moni," I objected.

"The two are also close friends."

Amused, I glanced at her from the side. "For not being a big fan of village gossip, you're pretty well informed!"

She shrugged her shoulders. "What are you supposed to do? You just get told whether you like it or not."

I understood what she meant. It was only my third day here and yet I already knew more about the people in the village than I did about my own neighbors. "You know what was strange? When I told her to protect me from Gregory's come-on, she completely shut down."

She nodded. "Rumor has it she had a thing with him once."

"No! Not really, is it?"

She shrugged her shoulders again. "You're asking the wrong person. If you don't want to hear rumors, but truths, ask Moni. She knows everything that goes on here, before and behind closed doors. But she doesn't tell everyone, she's very secretive, which is probably why everyone trusts her. Because secrets are safe with her. And believe me, there are enough of them here, precisely because there's so much talk. Besides, I told you that he's very popular and has been with almost all the girls."

"I'm definitely not going to be next!"

"Then watch out for him!" she laughed amusedly.

We stopped and got out. It was still light and we were standing on a small hill. That's when I saw it for the first time since I had been here - the ocean! As always, when I saw it again after a long time, I held my breath.

Smelled it, heard it and felt it.

The majestic expanse, the blue of the water that was lost in the sky; this freedom! It felt as if I had left the earth and was flying.

"Do you like it?" She regarded me from the side with a smile.

"Yes, it's beautiful," I said emotionally. Whenever, I came to the sea, I felt a strong longing for this wonderful blue landscape. One glance at the water, the sound of the surf; sand under my feet and I was immediately deeply relaxed. I slowly took my gaze off the sea and let it wander. A white sandy beach lined the shore as far as the eye could reach.

"That's where the movie theater is!" She pointed down to the left and I spotted a small clearing in the woods with a stretched screen and lots of chairs in front of it. It already looked well attended. "And there's the beach bar where we're going to the party tomorrow." She pointed now down to the beach, and sure enough, there was a building there.

"It's right by the ocean!" I exclaimed delightedly.

"Of course, that's why it's called a beach bar!" she teased me.

We followed a path that wound its way down through the forest. The trees rustled in the wind around us. The air smelled so fresh and clear that I realized I had completely forgotten how good it actually smelled. Was Marcello there yet? My heart was beating faster. "Excited?" she asked with a smile.

"Oh no, why should I?" I tried to play it off.

"After all, you have a date tonight. Oh, sorry, two dates!" she grinned.

"Nice of you to remind me," I muttered grimly. A path branched off to the left. There was a small hut on the corner and we headed towards it. "Where does it go straight on?" I asked curiously.

"Well, to the beach bar!"

We reached the little cottage. "Twice, Benjamin." She handed a bill inside.

"Right away," came the reply. A guy as old as us peeked out and caught sight of me. His face lit up with a beaming smile. "Hi, we met in the tunnel yesterday! I'm Benjamin!"

"Kathleen." I shook his hand, which he held out to me. He seemed totally unfamiliar, in the tunnel yesterday? I thought hard, that's right! Marcello and Gregory had been there and the third person was apparently him. "And you work here as well as your job?"

He smiled again enchantingly and handed her the change. "This isn't work, it's my hobby. I built it myself!" he added proudly.

"Wow, impressive!" I dug out my wallet. "I can't wait to see that! How much are you getting?"

"You're invited, come!" She grabbed my hand and pulled me with her.

"Claudia, that's really out of question!" I protested.

"What did I tell you earlier? Don't be unkind! Thank me and don't say much about it."

"Thank you!" I said obediently, did I have a choice?

Something moved behind the trees - my heart was pounding! Was it Marcello waiting for me? A person stepped out my pulse calmed down again. "Hello you pretty ladies!"

"Hello Gregory!" I mumbled, annoyed. He kissed her left and right on the cheek and before I knew it, he was doing the same to me, which annoyed me to no end!

He didn't seem to notice at all and grinned at me. "See, I told you she was coming today!" he said nonchalantly.

"Hmm," was my answer.

"I've saved you seats, c'mon!"

"I'm already sitting next to Marcello!"

"Yes, I know, he's sitting with us."

"Uh-huh." Great, what else could I say? Claudia couldn't stop grinning. We followed him and I punched her lightly in the side. We walked through a row of trees and stood in the clearing, which seemed even bigger than before from the hill. Almost all the chairs were occupied. He walked purposefully to one of the front rows, I kept an eye out for Marcello but couldn't find him anywhere.

"After you." He stood next to the third row of chairs, really good seats, as I reluctantly had to admit. Claudia stepped past him into the row. I looked around but only saw strange faces and no Marcello.

"Where's Marcello?"

"He's getting popcorn, c'mon!" he said impatiently, and I already had his hand on my back, pushing me into the line.

I freed myself. "Fine, I was just about to get some too!" And off I went.

"He gets enough for everyone!"

"Great, I'll help him carry it then!" I called over my shoulder and quickened my pace. Had he actually touched me? Dared to push me into the row of chairs? He was out of his mind, idiot!

I was so annoyed that I was suddenly standing in the middle of the woods again. Only now did I realize that I had no idea where the stupid popcorn was. I marched to the right, but somehow the forest became denser, it seemed to me. By now Marcello was surely back! So, I turned around and trudged straight ahead. But I must have done something wrong because I didn't get to the clearing! Maybe I had gone too far to the right earlier and just walked past it? So, I hurried to the left, but there were only trees there too. And wasn't I running in circles now? Hadn't the movie already begun, why didn't I hear anything? I was starting to get nervous, please, not again! I found it terrible to get lost and yet it kept happening to me! And in this big forest everything looked exactly the same! I could wander around in circles for hours and still never find my way out! Panic rose in me, why couldn't I hear the others? All I could hear were these stupid nature sounds! Birds chirping, the creaking and groaning of the trees, the rustling of the leaves. I started to run! I was about to cry for help, and felt stupid!

Then something big and dark burst out of the bushes - I screamed! Terrified, I held my arms in front of my face! When I took it down, Marcello stood in front of me smiling. "Well, slightly missed the popcorn stand?"

How embarrassing! And then my heart was beating so fast! It was all down to the excitement of getting lost, for sure! "No, I wanted to stretch my legs a bit," I replied proudly. "But we can go back now!" I walked straight ahead with determination.

His hand came to rest on my shoulder and held me back, he stepped close behind me. "That's the wrong direction," he whispered in my ear; a shiver running down my spine.

"I know, just wanted to test you!" I felt his hot breath on my neck, so close as he stood behind me. My whole body glowed! I turned around and met his tiger eyes - dangerous, wild and sensual.

"Kathleen, I've missed you!" he sighed and stroked my hair gently.

"Me too!" I blushed.

He took my hand, his eyes shone at me. He kissed me tenderly; first on one cheek, then on the other. His lips approached my mouth, they met, we kissed. It was just as fantastic as yesterday - I just loved it so much! I hugged him, snuggled up to him. He put his hands securely around my waist and pulled me gently against him. Then he let go of me and took my face in his hands, slowly I opened my eyes. "You're so beautiful, Kathleen!" he said softly, covering my face with sweet little kisses and stroking my back tenderly. I enjoyed it; he could go on like this forever! "And have you recovered from the shock yesterday?"

"What shock?"

He broke away from me, too bad, and smiled at me - so cute! "That I'm a tiger?"

"Oh that? Yeah, sure!" I grinned; he kissed me again. I stroked his arms, they were nice and soft, hairy ... hairy? I paused and stared at them; they were covered in black fur! "Aha! Then I wasn't imagining it the other day when we said goodbye at the Father's with your hand! It looked just like that!"

He glanced at it now, too. The hair disappeared and his soft dark human skin reappeared, he laughed embarrassedly. "Sorry, I can't control that. It happens when I get angry or when I have strong emotions."

"And are you angry now?" I asked him quietly and moved closer to him, our lips touching lightly.

"No," he replied just as quietly.

"Then what are you?" We kissed.

"Totally crazy about you!"

I smiled. The next kiss. "And why is that?" Two more kisses followed.

"Because I like you so much, Kathleen!" I noticed with excitement that his arms were covered in fur again! He opened his eyes, his gaze met mine and exploded inside me! We kissed for an eternity.

Then we let go of each other, breathless, and I stroked his furred arms. "Do you like that?" he asked with a smile.

I nodded. "Is it like that all over your body?"

"Yes, that's it."

"On your chest too?" I gently stroked his shirt and he sighed softly. "May I see it?" He nodded. Eagerly I opened the top button, black fur glistened from underneath and stroked it carefully. It was thick and dense and yet soft. He held my hand tightly, his pupils had narrowed and looked like a cat's or a tiger's. A small black dot and yellow around it, it fascinated me.

"No more, please," he begged, turning away and buttoning his shirt. Tiger or not, he was also a man and obviously full of passion.

"Can I ask you something, something intimate?" I said hesitantly. He turned to me, but was still looking at his shirt and fiddling with the button.

"Of course, always!"

"Are you turning into a tiger when you, you know?" I blushed slightly and he shook his head.

"No, I'm staying human." He glanced at me; his eyes were back to normal. "But I have fur all over and my pupils change shape and my eyes turn yellow."

"I just saw that."

"Yes? I'm not surprised," he smiled shyly. "I hope you like hairy men?" he asked worriedly; I laughed.

"I prefer a smooth body, but you don't have hair, you have thick fur. It feels smooth and quite soft. That's different from hair, it's nice." He smiled with relief. "It's like a cuddly toy!" I said happily and he grimaced.

"Cuddly toy?" he asked doubtfully.

"Yes!" I nodded enthusiastically. "I had a little black cuddly toy panther that felt the same! Although it was even softer and cuddlier."

He shook his head in horror. "No one ever said I was a cuddly toy!" He looked really unhappy and I gave him a friendly nudge.

"I didn't say you were a cuddly toy. Just that your fur feels a bit cuddly, okay?"

"Hm." He stood there with his arms folded and I kissed him on the cheek in a conciliatory manner.

"My strong tiger!" I whispered. Now he was smiling contentedly again and grinning. Men were so vulnerable in their ego; he was just like any other guy. We kissed again and I lightly stroked his cheek with the back of my fingers. "Can I ask you something else?"

"Always Kathleen! Ask anything you want to know!"

"Do you have fur on your face when you do, you know what?" I continued to stroke his cheek. During the kissing, I had opened my eyes every now and then, expecting to stroke a furry face, but that wasn't the case.

He nodded. "But only if I completely lose control of myself. Then I'll have fur on my face and my nose will also get wider and become a real tiger's nose." He looked down embarrassed at the floor and then glanced up ashamed. "But that only happens, you know, when you get to the end. Then I can't stop it. Do you find that repulsive?"

"I don't think so. As long as you remain human and no razor-sharp teeth suddenly gape out of your mouth?" I tried to make it sound more casual than I actually meant.

He took my hands. Held them in his between our bodies and peered at me insistently. "Kathleen, I have never and will never hurt a human being. And no, I have fur but no predator's teeth. You don't need to be afraid of me." He tenderly stroked a strand of hair from my face. "I would never hurt you. Although I'm no cuddly toy either." He hissed softly, his eyes glinting playfully. Maybe it was this moment. In any case, it was this mixture of danger and familiarity; of love and passion; of macho and loving partner. I fell in love with him and couldn't help it any more than he could, whose arms became furry again when we continued kissing. He stroked down my back, when our gazes met, I smiled. His eyes had become tiger eyes again.

At some point I could barely recognize him and glanced around. It had suddenly become quite dark! He smiled at me. "Shall we go?"

"Yes, we should! Otherwise, we won't be able to find our way back when it's pitch black!"

"You don't need to be afraid. I can also see in the dark. As you know, I'm a tiger, which also has advantages that you humans don't have!" He took my hand and we strolled off.

"For example?"

"My senses are much sharper! As a tiger I see, hear and smell more intensely and from a huge distance. Plus, I don't freeze thanks to my fur and water runs off me."

"That's why you don't mind the rain!"

"Exactly! I can also run really fast! I'm very strong and can carry heavy loads; jump far and climb well. By the way, that's how I found you here in the forest and down in the tunnel - I smelled you!"

"Well, thank you!"

He laughed, sniffed my neck and kissed me, giving me goose bumps. "Mmh ... I love your smell! I'd always find you!" he murmured ecstatically, which was very practical as I was always getting lost.

"Does that mean you can hear and see that far now?"

"No, I do that as a tiger. As a human, I'm just like you, probably even weaker."

"Weaker?"

"My true form is the tiger. As a human I use up a lot of energy and strength. As a tiger, I can use all my strength because I don't have to pretend. I am then myself and can use all my abilities and be who I am meant to be."

"Then why are you so often a human? You should only be out and about as a tiger," I replied indignantly.

"Oh yeah?" he laughed. "I'm glad that my friends accept me for who I am. I'm as much of a tiger as I can be, but otherwise I adapt to society. I like being alone, but I also need the company. That's why I looked for you as a tiger and found you as a human." I remembered the large dark shadow that had broken through the bushes and scared me so much.

"So, you were out as a tiger earlier when you were looking for me?" He nodded. "And turned yourself into a human for my sake, which drained your strength and energy?"

He nibbled on my ear. "Don't worry, I've got plenty of it!"

"But if you only have your skills as a tiger, how do you know we're going right?"

"Oh babe." He hugged me from behind as we walked and kissed my ear. So of course, we barely made any progress. "I still have the human sense of direction though. And since you just walked in the absolute opposite direction from the movie theater, the way back is pretty easy. Just straight back!"

I shook him off. "It can't be!"

"Oh, no?" He grinned at me; I could sense it more than see it. Now that the sun had set, it became dark in one fell swoop.

"Because I always turned right, we should have always gone left. Oh Marcello, I can hardly see you anymore! We set off too late and are now walking straight into the darkness! We'll never get to the cinema!"

"Shh ... can't you hear anything?"

I listened and sure enough - I heard music and voices! He grabbed me from behind again, by now it was completely dark around us, reached forward and bent branches out of our way.

Suddenly we were back in the clearing! In front of us were the chairs with all the spectators and behind us the screen was flickering. "Come!" he whispered and took my hand. In the light of the projector, we scurried to the last row of chairs where there was still a free seat. He sat down and pulled me onto his lap.

"We are way too late! The movie started a long time ago!" I whispered. "The others will miss us and wonder where we've been for so long!"

"That long?" he amused himself. "I've been sitting here in this chair with you the whole time! So, when it's break time, we can go to them and tell them."

"A break? Are you sure?"

"Yes, because Benjamin has to change the movie reels." He sank his nose into my hair.

"What kind of movie is this anyway?"

"It doesn't matter," he murmured contentedly from my hair.

I was trying to focus on the movie when the screen went black with "PAUSE" written in big letters. "Marcello, you're right! It's intermission!" There was a murmur of voices around us and we moved from our seats. "Wasn't I too heavy for you?"

He laughed. "I could easily put up with you on my lap all evening, let's go!" He led me safely through the corridor to the front. He could say what he liked, but it seemed to me that his senses were sharper than those of normal people. Just now in the woods, you really couldn't see anything at the end. And I had only spotted the wandering mouse on our walk yesterday when it scurried past our feet, whereas he had discovered it much earlier. He pushed me into the line and I inched my way past the knees and tucked-up legs of the others.

"Sorry!" I mumbled, but no one seemed to mind, it was break time anyway. Our seats were in the middle. I passed Gregory and was very glad that Marcello had guided me into the row first. So, to my delight, I sat next to Claudia and he sat next to him! Well, tough luck, dear Gregory!

"Kathleen! There you are! Are you all right?" she exclaimed with relief.

"Yes, everything's fine! We were sitting at the back. We didn't want to disturb everyone, that's why we only came to the front now." That wasn't entirely true. But on the other hand, it was nobody's business what we had been doing in the forest for so long. We sat down.

"Tiger, this is Kathaleena's place!" Gregory grumbled.

Marcello looked at me questioningly, I shook my head. Satisfied, he smiled. "I'm sitting here now!" he said determinedly.

"Do you still have any popcorn?" I asked, a bag was handed to me from the left.

I held it out to him, he declined. "I don't eat that kind of food. It's for you!"

Gregory didn't admit defeat yet. He leaned forward and peeked past him to me. "And Kathaleena, how do you like the movie?" he asked eagerly.

"Good, funny!"

"Funny?" He frowned. Oh dear, that had obviously been wrong, it was probably a drama!

"I mean, it was funny at first. But afterwards I thought it got sad," I tried to talk my way out of it.

"Sad?" he continued to wonder.

"You know, that thing at the end."

"The adoption?"

"Yes, that's exactly what I mean. It's a bit sad when you think about it, isn't it?"

"Hm," he said.

"How do you like the movie?" I asked back, before things got even more awkward.

"Exciting! What do you think will happen with the little one?"

"The little one?"

"Well, the girl, if you can call her that, who they've adopted." Ah, it was probably a movie about a gender change about a girl who felt like a boy.

"I just hope she will be happy in her life!" This answer simply couldn't be wrong, it was universally valid! However, his mouth remained open, speechless. "Do you disagree?" I asked.

"Yeah, I think they'll shoot her and the other kids too!" Now my mouth was hanging open! What kind of movie was that in which children were shot? "What do you mean, Tiger?" Somehow, it gave me a twinge that he called him Tiger. It was such a private secret part of him and he made it an everyday thing.

Marcello shrugged his shoulders. I grinned, now he would embarrass himself too. "I think everyone dies in the end," he said calmly; Gregory nodded.

"I think so too or everyone else dies and the kids get away with it!"

"Or the others die first and then, as a surprise, the kids die too!"

"That's it, tiger!" He enthusiastically slapped him on the shoulder. "You've got it out again!"

Offended, I leaned back. Great, why was he right? He hadn't seen the movie either! Claudia smirked. "What is it?" I asked innocently.

"So, so, you think the movie is funny?" she chuckled.

"Yes, why not? Don't you?"

"You can call it funny, sure. I just didn't know you were into movies like that. Well then, laugh out loud at the amusing parts!"

"I'll do that all the time, you'll see!"

"I'm excited! Oh, it goes on!" She leaned back with pleasure; the screen flickered.

I would definitely laugh out loud! There were funny parts in every movie, it wouldn't be that serious! I cuddled up to Marcello. He wrapped his arm around me and laid his head against mine - it was so cozy! He stroked my back lovingly and I stroked his. I would have loved to kiss him again, but I didn't want to put on a show in front of Gregory. We could always do that later when we were alone. I glanced up at the sky, countless stars twinkled above us. It was really different from sitting in a closed movie theater. Trees enveloped us protectively, the light from the screen reflected on their leaves; it looked like a painting.

I focused on the movie. Sure enough, it was about a little innocent girl who had been adopted and I thought Gregory was just morbid to wish her dead! The sweet child was home alone with the babysitter. Suddenly, without any warning, it ripped the sitter's head off! I screamed in horror and hid in Marcello's shoulder, but he must have found the scene quite funny. No wonder, he saw enough blood during his hunt and stroked my head reassuringly. "Can I look again?" I asked.

"Hm, not yet," he said calmly. Since he sounded so cool, I risked a glance and quickly turned away. The girl was gnawing on the sitter's bloody arm! And so, it went on! There were other adopted children who were all monsters in reality and they ate their way through anything that moved. I spent most of the time in Marcello's shoulder, but he laughed now and then and Gregory roared in approval. No wonder he was surprised that I found it funny when it was a horror film! I thought it was disgusting and brutal! In the end, it happened as Marcello had predicted. After the remaining villagers dug in and the monsters entered to eat them, a bomb went off. The villagers had planted it and gathered there as human bait, in a sense, to lure the monsters in and wipe them out completely.

After the movie I felt slightly nauseous, it really wasn't my genre! So, I was glad when it was finally over and we got up and left. "Ah, how good that we're driving home now!" I murmured to Claudia.

"Do you want to go home already?" she asked.

I looked at her surprised. "Do you have any other plans?"

"Everyone's heading to the Father's now. But if you'd rather want to go home, we don't have to join them."

"Father's sounds good! I'm just glad the movie's over!"

She smiled. "Must have been too funny for you."

"Yes, although it was a bit sad at the end."

"Because the poor girl didn't get happy," she added with a grin.

"Exactly!" I shouted. Somehow, I had lost Marcello on the way out. But when we got to the hut, he was standing there waiting for me, restlessly stepping from one leg to the other. "Marcello!" I called out happily. "Are you coming to the Father's?" He nodded.

"I'll go ahead!" Claudia smiled conspiratorially at me.

He stepped behind the hut where Benjamin had sat earlier and collected the entrance fee; now it was empty. I followed him so that people could walk past us unhindered. He looked pale and had his hands clasped in his upper arms. "Are you all right?" I asked anxiously and wanted to touch him, but he pulled away.

"Yes." His voice sounded rough. "I'll come to the Father's later." I was a little disappointed. Somehow, I had assumed that he was going there with us. "See you then!" He turned around abruptly.

"Wait!" I grabbed him by the arm, he pushed me back! I gazed at him shocked.

"Sorry." He disappeared behind the trees.

I stood alone by the hut; everyone had left the movie theater. Slowly I climbed up the path, what had that been? He had actually left me alone in the woods! I wasn't used to anything like that from him! He was always a gentleman and courteous and then he had pushed me! I was stunned, but there was something wrong with him! He seemed completely distraught. What I didn't understand, though, was that first he waited for me and then pushed me and left me standing there? I was starting to get angry! After all, I had asked him what was wrong and he had replied that everything was fine! And yet, somehow, he had been different. He had been totally energized! As if he was going to burst at any moment and pull himself together with all his might.

I arrived upstairs; Claudia was sitting in the car. I opened the passenger door in a huff and got in. She started the engine. "And was there another kiss goodbye?" she asked with a wink.

"No!" I blurted out. "There was a goodbye push!"

"Push?" We drove off. The car jolted along the uneven forest floor until we hit asphalt.

I held on to the seat. "Yes! He wanted to tell me that he would join us later in the Father's. And when he wanted to leave and I grabbed him, he pushed me away!"

"How shameless!"

"Yes, isn't it!"

She shook her head. "I don't know him like that," she said indignantly.

"I was horrified too!" It did me good that she agreed with me! "And he didn't want to come with us either!"

"Although I don't think he ever rides in the car, he prefers to walk. As far as I've heard. I haven't had that much to do with him yet." She turned off.

"Still, he could at least have accompanied me to the car! Instead, I had to find my way up alone in the dark!"

"Well, I'll tell him something later in the Father's! How dare he!" she said enraged.

"But somehow, he looked totally messed up, almost sick. He was pale all over!"

"He didn't seem that sick during the movie that he wouldn't have wanted to accompany you. I think he didn't feel like it!" she continued angrily.

It was funny, it was actually exactly what I had thought! But the more she expressed my opinion, the more I started to want to defend him. "But then why was he waiting for me? He could have told Gregory that he was running late."

"Wait for you and then leave you standing there? You can do without that!"

"Yes, but something was wrong with him."

"Obviously! No normal man leaves a woman alone in the woods at night!"

I didn't answer that and so we drove on to the Father's in silence, me chewing nervously on my lower lip and trying to make sense of his behavior. When we got out, I turned around and watched out for Father Mountain. Indeed, I recognized its dark outline against the night sky, which was not so dark in comparison. The stars were twinkling all over the firmament, just like yesterday on our night walk. Why was he late, did he want to go home and change?

We entered; it was packed. All the seats were taken, Moni was dashing around the room at a monkey's pace and there were still people standing around everywhere. In contrast to the quiet night just outside, there was a nightclub atmosphere here.

"Hey!" Gregory had spotted us straight away and waved. The bad thing was that he was the only one I knew here to some extent. It was probably the same for Claudia, because we made our way to him and he was there straight away, kissing us left and right as usual. "What do you want to drink?" he asked.

"A Coke," I replied, she took a beer.

"Benny! A Coke and a beer for the ladies!" he shouted. That was typical! Instead of placing the order with Moni himself, he passed it on to poor Benjamin! As if he hadn't already done enough today after his shift in the mountain and the movie screening! But then Benjamin came rushing up, holding a tray and serving drinks. He handed me the Coke and Claudia the beer and ran back to the bar, where he picked up a new tray.

I gazed after him astonished. "Does he work here?"

"Who?" Claudia took a sip of the beer and glanced in Gregory's direction.

"Well, Benjamin!"

"Oh, him. Yes, he helps out here after the movie. Since everyone comes here straight on, Moni can't do it alone with all the orders." Benjamin was already at the bar again, picking up a new tray. Moni was busy tapping beer, impressive!

Gregory's heated face blocked my view of him. "C'mon, Kathaleena, let'ssssss have a toast!" We clinked glasses. He drank his half-full beer mug in one go, I sipped my Coke. He swayed slightly, shouted, "Benny, a beer!" and turned to me again. "You're a reeeeeeal sweetie, you know that?"

Being hit on so drunk and then also with such standard come-ons totally turned me off! Why on earth was Marcello late and left me here unprotected to his pick-up buddy! Then I had an idea. "Gregory, can I ask you something?"

He pulled me onto his shoulder and put his arm heavily around me. Because I wanted to know something from him, I let him. "Allllwaysssss, sweetie! Anything you want!"

"It's because of Marcello. He was totally weird after the movie! Said, he'd come later and just left."

He nodded. "Yes, you don't know him. But you have to understand that he's a tiger, an animal. And the movie made him nervous."

"The movie?" I couldn't understand that his behavior had anything to do with that!

"Yes, all that blood! The hunting and killing! Tiger is a hunter. That incited him!"

"Incited?" I asked, still not understanding what he was trying to tell me. I broke free from his embrace to look at him directly. "What do you mean by that?"

He sighed. "It turned him on, made him hot, awakened his instinct!"

"And that means?"

"That he has to go hunting nooooow!"

"But he just went yesterday!"

He shrugged his shoulders. "He's not going to hunt anything big. He's not interested in eating today. He's not interested in satisfying his physical hunger. He has a different hunger to satisfy!" He seemed to enjoy his lecture, theatrically he continued, "Today he hunts for the thrill, the desire to kill!" I stared at him, stunned. He held both his hands in front of me and with a snarling sound let one jump on the other and clenched his fist tightly around it as if he wanted to crush it. "Do you understand?" He turned around. "Benny! Where's my beer?"

And I understood! Wheeled around and just wanted to get out! I fought my way through the many bodies standing between me and the door. Finally got there, pulled it open and was outside in the cool night air! I only had one image in mind - it was the scene from the movie when I had taken a peek. But now I didn't see the little girl gnawing on the babysitter's arm, but Marcello! Who tore off the head and feasted on the body! Chewing the flesh off the corpse with his teeth and eating it, filled with murderous desire! Blood covering his hands and skin! I felt so sick I was going to throw up and put my hand over my mouth.

The door opened. "Kathleen? Are you all right?" I just shook my head silently. "What is it?" Claudia stepped up next to me and put her arm around me. "You're all pale! What's happened? Did the air in there get to you?"

The nausea slowly subsided and I dared to speak. "I talked to Gregory and asked him about Marcello and he's coming later because he's hunting. But not because he's hungry, but because the movie turned him on and now, he wants to feel the thrill of the kill!" I hadn't been able to make it sound as dramatic as Gregory, but I thought it was violent enough as it was.

"He might catch a rabbit," she reassured me.

"Claudia!" I stared at her. "You don't understand! He's a killer! A murderer! A ..."

"Predator," she said calmly. "I know. And predators hunt other animals."

"But he's so sweet and kind! How can he be so cruel and murderous?"

"He will certainly eat the game he hunts. He doesn't just do it for fun."

"Yes, that's exactly what he's doing today!" I looked at her seriously.

"It's his instinct. He has to hunt; he can't help it! But afterwards he will eat the prey. It's not the animals that kill other animals that are cruel, it's the people who hunt them! They are filled with a lust for murder and the urge to kill! And they don't even stop at their own kind. They only kill to hang a trophy on their wall or out of greed, revenge;

jealousy and envy. Marcello, on the other hand, is pure of heart. He only does it to make a living, to survive."

I shook my head. "That's exactly it! Today he hunts as a human! Not as an animal! He's not hungry at all, he's just incited!"

"If he eats a rabbit today, next time he will only need a small animal. His stomach is not like ours. He can fill his belly and live on it for days, while we need food every day. If he hunts more often, the prey will be smaller. But he'll still only catch exactly what he needs to live, no more. That's why it's totally fine, because it remains in balance. The animals are in harmony with each other with nature. It's the humans who upset the balance with their greed and excess, not the animals! And of course, he has this instinct to hunt and kill, he is a tiger after all! And when he sees a movie like today, which is all about that, it's no wonder that his hunting instinct is awakened and stimulated." She took a deep breath.

"So, you don't think it's bad!" I gave her a disappointed glance.

"No," she replied simply.

"You don't think it's bad that he roams the woods in a murderous mood?"

"I think you're exaggerating."

"And you're playing it down! What if a wanderer comes along the path and he attacks him in his murderous rage?"

She stared at me. "So that's what it's about, I see. You think he's hurting people!"

"It can't be ruled out if he's in that mood, can it?" Now she looked disappointed. "What's wrong? Am I not right?" I asked, humorlessly she laughed briefly.

"You know what's strange? That's exactly what his father always told us all! Why he doesn't go public, for example, but keeps himself and his special nature a secret. I didn't understand it back then when he said they would see him as a threat. He was the most peaceful person I have ever met. Friendly, helpful, willing to compromise, calming disputes, we all loved him. He had such a sunny disposition! If someone was feeling bad, he always had the right words to comfort them. And if there was a problem, he had the solution. He was appreciated, respected and admired. And so, no one understood why he thought that if he went public, people would lock him up and fear him. After all, who would fear or even want to imprison such a kind, loving man who couldn't harm anyone? But now you come along and say exactly what he has always told us. So, he was right again."

I didn't know what to say to that. We both fell silent and gazed out into the clear air.

After a while, she said coolly, "Well, I'm going back inside, see you later."

I nodded and stood outside alone again. Had she been right about what she was accusing me of? Was I really afraid that he would hurt people? Was I afraid that he would hurt me? But she was right about one thing, he was a predator. He would always hunt; he would have to. If I wanted to love him, I would have to respect that side of him. Whether I liked it or not, whether it scared me or not. And hadn't he promised me earlier that he had never hurt anyone and never would and that I didn't need to be afraid of him? But those were words and the feeling in my stomach was different - I was scared! Scared of him, in this mood. He had pushed me today, what would it be next time? And I didn't like that he enjoyed killing, hunting. I ate meat too, but only to satisfy my hunger. I liked it too, but I had no desire to hunt and kill an animal! If I had to,

I would become a vegetarian immediately! No, I didn't understand this instinct. I also didn't understand the human hunters who just had pure fun shooting the poor animals and went hunting with their weapons. And so, Marcello also eluded my understanding and therefore my acceptance.

Then I noticed a movement from a distance, which became a person coming closer. It was him, he smiled at me. "I knew it was you, I smelled you from a long way off!"

I remained silent. He was now standing right in front of me and I felt nothing but disgust for him. Yes, it really was a disguise! This innocent human form he was wearing. Like the children in the movie, who were innocent and pure, but in reality monsters. But like this, in the children shape, they lulled their prey into a false sense of security. Only to attack them when they were completely defenseless and unprotected.

He frowned. "What's going on?" he asked sharply.

"Had fun?" I asked curtly.

"I went hunting."

"I know, Gregory told me. You didn't seem to be in the right mood to tell me earlier, or even more so not to tell me."

"What's wrong?" he asked gently.

I wanted him to leave! It was easier to loathe him when he wasn't standing in front of me. But this way I could see his loving gaze, his confused face and felt his sadness that he didn't understand me. I would just say it out loud, then he would understand. "Gregory said you didn't go hunting today to satisfy your hunger, but for the thrill. For the thrill of the kill." I glanced at him challengingly, he hesitated.

"It's true that I wasn't hungry, but I can eat even when I'm not. And yes, hunting gives me a kick. But I have no desire to kill." He now looked me straight in the eye. "I like hunting and I live off what I kill. But I have no desire or pleasure in killing, it just comes from hunting. It's more ..." He seemed to be struggling for the right words, I waited. "It's more like a game. It's the risk, it's the effort I put in! I have to wait, lurk and then strike at the right moment." He stopped because he met my petrified expression. "I can't explain it to you," he said, defeated. "All I know is that I have to do it at moments like this or I'll burst."

"And hurt people?" Now it was out! I held my breath tensely.

His gaze changed from hurt and struck to angry and then disappointed. "I told you, I will never and have never attacked or hurt anyone. Neither me nor my father," he said quietly.

"But you're not ruling out that it could happen, are you?" I asked challengingly.

He regarded me sadly. "I can say what I want now. You already have your answer that you believe in." He walked past me.

I heard the door open behind me, voices came rushing out, then it closed and it was silent. I had rarely felt so alone in my life before. I went out onto the grass, crouched down on the ground and cried. Slowly the tears dried up, leaving only this emptiness inside me that I knew all too well. Did I just think that I had rarely felt so alone in my life? That wasn't true. I had just forgotten or wanted to forget this feeling of loneliness and emptiness. Sure, there were my friends in the city who asked how I was doing. But still, when I stood next to them, I always felt somehow alone and misunderstood. I laughed with them, went out with them and yet I was still lonely. The people around me merged into a unit. They understood each other, laughed together, had their topics of conversation. But I was outside, excluded, as if I didn't belong. When I went out with my friends in the city and now here. What was I doing wrong? Everyone made it, became friends and I was there and yet I wasn't. Basically, it was like it was right now. Everyone was partying inside and I was sitting outside alone and didn't belong. But where and to whom did I belong? There was nothing that really meant anything to me in my life. I was living and doing my duties and sometimes I forgot about this emptiness and loneliness. If I just did enough, it was easy to distract myself from the feeling. To run away from it, to block it out. But then there were moments like now. Nothing to distract me and no matter where I went, I took myself with me. And no matter how far I ran away from me, at some point I caught up with myself. No matter how many activities I filled my life with, at some point there was a gap and then I came to rest. And felt myself and I consisted of this great emptiness and loneliness. No matter how many blankets I could have wrapped myself in, nothing could dispel the cold inside me. But when the fire of love blazed inside me, as it did with Marcello, it was gone. Then I was completely filled with him and his love and my love for him. Oh Marcello, why are you just being a tiger?

The door was opened. Voices and laughter floated out as if from another world to which I had no access. Footsteps approached. I turned around shyly, but only saw a slender male figure against the Father's lighted windows. "Coke?" He held out a glass to me.

"Benjamin?" I asked, he laughed softly.

"Hi! Sorry, you can't see much when you look against the light, can you?" He stood sideways now, the Father's light flooding his fine face. "That's better?" he asked.

"Yes, thank you." What was I supposed to say to that, what was he doing out here? Had they sent him out to check on me?

He sat down next to me on the grass and carefully put down the glass, which I hadn't taken from him. He lay down, stretched and moaned with pleasure. "Does that feel good." He rolled onto his side, propped his elbow up and rested his chin on his hand. I glanced ahead and was really not in a chatty mood. The last two people I'd talked to had been so disappointed that they'd left me. "I always come out here to catch my breath, too," he said.

"Hm," I replied.

"Whenever Moni allows me to." He laughed quietly again and I kept quiet. He was supposed to leave! Go in and say, "I'm sorry, I tried everything! Brought her something to drink, had a nice, non-committal chat with her. But she didn't want to talk to me either! There's nothing we can do."

Then Marcello and Claudia would reply, "Don't worry, it's not you. You just can't talk to her!"

The door opened again. Aha, so he had gone, I turned around, relieved. But he was still lying next to me in the grass, now on his back again.

"Here you are!" I heard a voice that had become very familiar to me against my will. Gregory groaned and sat down next to me on the other side, was there nowhere to rest? Did I look like I wanted company? Wasn't that why I was sitting alone outside in the dark?

"Do I have to go back inside?" yawned Benjamin.

"I don't think so. Otherwise, Moni would already be calling. But she's got everything under control, it looks like." Gregory burped. "Sorry," he chuckled and Benjamin laughed.

"As if you could objectively judge anything now!"

"I can! For example, that Kathaleena has nothing left to drink!"

Before Benjamin could protest, I picked up the Coke glass. Still facing forward, I tried to ignore the two boys, at least visually. "I've still got enough!"

"Ah," Gregory was surprised.

"You see, you have no overview at all," Benjamin teased as the door opened again.

"Hey, are you guys having a private party here?"

I half-turned, three figures came towards us.

"Cool, Bobby! Come here, play us something on your guitar!" Gregory bellowed.

It was all getting too much for me! If I had wanted people around me, I would have gone back inside. I stood up, annoyed, and Benjamin was standing next to me.

"Will you accompany me for a while?" he asked me quietly. By now the other three were sitting down and the one Gregory had called Bobby actually had a guitar with him and started strumming a few chords. Somehow, he seemed familiar to me, but I couldn't figure out where.

I didn't want to do anything with Benjamin, but I didn't want to get lost again and have to be rescued by Marcello. Marcello ... a heavy stone grew in my stomach. "Okay," I said, slowly we started walking.

"Hey Benny, where are you going, you womanizer!" Gregory called after us.

"Stretch my legs a bit, see you later!"

"Aren't you needed at the Father's?" I asked Benjamin. It sounded just like I meant it, that I wanted to get rid of him.

But he just laughed charmingly. "No, otherwise Moni would have brought me back in long ago."

Silently we strolled down the road. "Where does this path go?" I asked him after a while, feeling a little queasy, as I didn't know him at all.

"To the woods," he replied calmly.

"To the woods?" I asked in horror! What did he want me to do there? When I thought of the woods, I immediately thought of Marcello again. "Is that where Marcello goes hunting?"

"No, he hunts in a forest much further away from here." He fell silent. "I wish I was as free as he is," he said so quietly that I thought I'd misheard him.

"Free?" I regarded him from the side for the first time, not recognizing much. By now we were too far away from the Father's. The only light illuminating the way ahead came from the half moon above us and that wasn't much.

"Yes, Marcello is the freest person I know."

"What makes you think that?" I found Marcello quite the opposite. Hadn't he just said that he had to go hunting after a movie like that because otherwise he would burst? Being so dependent on his instincts and losing his temper seemed pretty unfree to me!

Benjamin sighed deeply. "He can live wherever he wants, just lie on the ground in the forest. Eat what he hunts down. He's independent of the weather, never gets sick. He's totally autonomous. Doesn't need a job to survive, has no obligations to anyone." His voice sounded longing. "He's his own boss. Can run wherever he wants, can cover long distances effortlessly. Do what he wants to do. Leave alone what he doesn't want. Nobody can force him to do anything. He is completely free and independent."

"Except for the small matter that he has to go hunting," I objected.

"We also have to eat, sleep and drink." He had become louder. "Those are basic needs. But he can eat when he wants, how much he wants and where he wants." He laughed softly.

"Yes, but he lives a life just like yours!" I was totally irritated. Somehow this Benjamin really seemed to have a burning heart when he thought about Marcello's life. "I mean, he lives in a house, I'm assuming. Works in mining, goes partying with you, he doesn't lead a different life! Apart from his eating habits." I shook myself with disgust at the thought.

"I know!" He shook his head. "I know he does. But if I were him ..." He fell silent and stopped, by now we had reached the edge of the forest.

I stopped too and looked around, the Father's was just a small glowing point of light in the distance. A cold wind blew, leaves rustled high above us. I shivered and turned back to him. "Yes? You in his place ...?" He shrugged his shoulders and seemed just as depressed as I felt. This made me realize that I had completely forgotten that I was down. "If I were him," I continued the sentence, "I would lead a normal life. I'd eat a normal steak and stop hunting."

Surprised, he glanced at me from the side and laughed. "Good job you're not a tiger then!"

I laughed at the idea too, then became serious again. "Benjamin, are you sometimes scared of him?"

He peered ahead towards the woods and shook his head. "Nah, why should I? I'm not a deer," he amused himself and turned around. "Shall we go back?"

"Yes." We started walking and somehow, I felt better. We didn't talk anymore, but there was no silence between us either, I liked him. I hadn't known him for long. But he was so pleasantly unobtrusive and I felt like I was completely myself next to him. I was sure that nothing I said would upset him. Hm ... and he was right, what was I afraid of? After all, I wasn't a deer either. "Do you hear that?" I asked him and he smiled. It was beautiful! Soft chords wafted towards us and wove themselves more and more into a melody the closer we got. "Tell me, do they sing?" He nodded. But it wasn't the bawling I'd expected from drunken village boys. They were clear and quite melodic voices, one singing voice totally stood out! It was bright and sounded so pure it sent a shiver down my spine. It effortlessly managed the complicated scale of the song and climbed even the highest notes with ease. I exhaled and only now realized that I had been holding my breath.

He was watching me from the side, now I could recognize him better. He had fine features, almost looked like a girl if I hadn't known otherwise, chin-length hair framing his face. "Do you like the voice?"

"Yes, it's beautiful, who's that?" I asked moved, he smiled knowingly.

We reached the Father's. A few bodies were lolling around on the floor. I kept an eye out for the super singer. What a talent, what a fine spirit he must be? What a sensitive tenor, what gentleness! I saw the guitarist Bobby and then I spotted the singer, his back turned to us! But was I wrong, or was it really him? But Gregory turned around. "Hey, there you are again!" he shouted delightedly. No doubt! That beautiful voice that I had just adored so much belonged to him! How could that be? "Have a seat!" Benjamin sat down next to him; Gregory moved a little away from him. He smiled invitingly at me and knocked at his side. I settled down between the two of them. He started singing again, I couldn't believe it and stared at him sideways. Goose bumps running down my arms,

I felt warm. Then the song was over. Everyone laughed in good spirits and a new one started. This time he unfortunately didn't sing along. "I'm sorry I scared you earlier, by the way. Because of Tiger." He regarded me with his blue eyes and seemed really embarrassed.

I slowly understood what Claudia meant by girls' crush - he wasn't ugly. "It's okay. Besides, you were right."

"Are you feeling better?" He was now watching me with real concern, which touched me deeply. He was the only one who didn't think I was stupid, he understood me! Marcello and Claudia hadn't! Instead, they had rejected me, were disappointed and had walked away from me! But he had come out to be with me! And he hadn't just checked if I was fine, I was pretty sure that he had been waiting for my return from the walk. I didn't need to justify myself to him. He put his arm around my shoulders and I let him. I had felt so lonely, it was so good to feel someone close! He kissed me on the hair - the door opened; I glanced up. A dark outline appeared briefly against the light doorway before it closed again. "Ah, Tiger. Why don't you join us?" he said casually and slid his arm down to my waist. I felt Marcello's shocked gaze as he looked at us and tried to release Gregory's arm from me, but he tightened his grip! Marcello shook his head, turned to the street and left.

I vigorously shook Gregory off and jumped up. "Marcello, wait!" I shouted, but he quickened his pace! I started to run! Suddenly I stumbled, lost my balance completely, cried out and fell forward! Strong arms caught me and I was in his arms - for a moment. Then he let go of me again, turned around and walked away. "Marcello, stop!" He didn't answer. I ran after him, grabbed him by the arm. He hissed and wheeled around, his dark eyes flashing. "Are you trying to scare me, Marcello?" I jutted my chin out at him. "Then forget it! I'm not afraid of you and you owe me a conversation!" Actually, he didn't owe me one, but I wanted him to talk to me! He wriggled out of my grip and before my eyes he turned into a black tiger. He hissed at me again, I saw his teeth, his claws on his paws! But then I met his eyes and they were Marcello's eyes with his hurt and offended look. A warm wave of affection washed through me. "I'm not afraid of you, Marcello," I said softly and stepped towards him. He stopped hissing and regarded me sadly. I lifted my hand, stroked his tiger head and smiled. His ears felt funny! Really like a cuddly toy, totally soft! Then I suddenly felt soft skin under my hand.

He had turned back into a human and was kneeling in front of me. He stood up, pushed my hand away and glared at me passionately. "I am a tiger! You can't change that!" he shouted.

"I know."

"You can't change me!"

"I know."

"I will always be a tiger! I will always hunt!" His eyes flashed at me challengingly.

"I know, Marcello."

His gaze changed, he now glanced at me tenderly and hurt. A renewed wave of affection flowed through me. "Oh Marcello, I know. I like you just the way you are!" I reached out to him and stroked his cheek gently.

He took it, kissed it and looked at me seriously. "Then why don't you accept me as a tiger?" he asked sadly.

"I accept you as a tiger, I really do. "

"Okay." He pulled me into his arms, I cuddled up to him and he stroked my back. I sensed that not everything was good between us yet, but maybe we just needed time to grow closer, as different as we were. Laughing voices approached. "Come!" He took me by the hand and we started walking until we were around the bend in the road. It was noticeably cooler here than in front of the Father's. A light wind was blowing and I shivered. "You're freezing!" He wrapped me in his arms again. I snuggled up to his warm body and felt so protected, as if nothing could ever happen to me again. "I'll take you home."

"That's too far to walk," I mumbled, as I had only driven back the distance yesterday with Ben in his car and that had been quite a distance.

He laughed. "Not if I take you with me, if you like?"

I glanced at him surprised. "Oh, you're here by car?"

He shook his head, let go of me and turned back into a tiger. It was really fascinating and happened so quickly! He had just been a human and suddenly there was a black tiger.

"C'mon, get on", I heard his voice in my head! How cool! So that's what he had meant by telepathic communication!

"What do you mean, get on?"

He stood close to me. "Sit on my back," I heard his voice inside me again.

"But, am I not too heavy for you?"

It looked like he was smiling. He shook his tiger head and regarded me in a friendly and inviting way with his tiger eyes. At that moment, he resembled more a big dog than a predator.

"Well then." Somehow, I felt a bit strange sitting on him, what was I going to tell my friends in the city? No one would understand! Yet now I was sitting on his broad tiger's back.

"Are you comfortable?"

"Yes, thank you."

"Lean forward a little and embrace my neck."

I did so carefully and wrapped my arms around him. "Do you often take girls home with you?" I imagined how other girls had also been on his back, hugging him, and I became jealous.

I heard a strange noise that sounded like a tiger laughing. "No, don't worry."

"Okay." I wouldn't have taken it from Gregory. But he would probably have said something like, "It happens from time to time, but you're special." or words similar to that. Why was I thinking about him now anyway? His sweet singing voice echoed inside me, I shook my head to drive it away and snuggled closer to Marcello.

"Hold on tight!" He ran a few steps, I was already wobbling back and forth and gripped him tighter. Then he sprinted off! Startled, I clung to him. The wind rushed past me, my hair fluttered. I pressed myself close to him and felt his muscles move smoothly beneath me, his body getting hotter and hotter and warming me. He dashed through the forest, the trees flew past us, it was pitch dark. I could only make out their outlines and often nothing at all. But he raced determinedly and without a moment's hesitation along the path that only he could see. I felt like I was flying! The steady rhythm of his movements calmed me and made me feel weightless. The soft ground beneath him cushioned his steps so that I was rocked softly and gently back and forth. I closed my eyes and enjoyed the feeling of being carried safely. Time seemed to stand still. Then the rhythm changed, he stopped, we had arrived. Too bad! It could have been a little longer. His body gave way beneath me, I lay in his arms. He lifted me up and carried me.

"Marcello! I'm much too heavy!"

He laughed. "You're light as a feather! I'm also strong." And as I was tired and had never been carried by a boy before, I let him. He put me down and we stood outside the front door.

"Thank you," I said and he smiled.

"With pleasure. I hope it was nice for you?"

"Yes, it was very nice!" He stroked my hair out of my face and I tried to smooth it down. "I'm probably all disheveled! I must look terrible!"

"You look beautiful!" He kissed me and took me in his arms.

"That was really wonderful, Marcello," I murmured happily.

"That's why I don't drive a car. I just get around like this."

"Yes, I understand that. And we were really fast, weren't we?"

"We're just as fast as a car, sometimes even faster! Because I take the direct route and we don't have any traffic lights."

"Traffic lights in the forest would be really stupid too," I laughed. "How did you find the way?"

"I have a pretty good sense of direction and I've already told you that as a tiger, my senses are much sharper than those of humans. That's how I hear and see my way."

"And then you're so strong too!"

He grinned. "I work in the mine; you build up a lot of muscle."

I snuggled up to his well-toned upper body. "Then you certainly don't need to diet."

"No, it's because of my tiger genes, I burn a lot of energy. But the others burn a lot at work too. None of us here need that. I certainly don't know anyone who does that."

"I am. All my friends are on a diet!" I grinned, then I remembered. "I'm on one too!"

"What for?" he asked in horror.

"I want to lose weight!"

He pushed me away and glanced at me seriously. "You're perfect the way you are, alright?"

"You might think so, but I'm a bit fat here and there."

"You're just making yourself crazy about other people! I'm telling you, you're perfect just the way you are!"

"And I'm telling you, I don't think so! And if I want to lose weight, that's my business!"

"It's not! Since you're my girlfriend, it's my business too!"

"First of all, we're not really together yet, we're still seeing each other! And then this is my body and my life and no matter what relationship I have with you, it will never be any of your business!"

He opened his mouth, but I rummaged in my handbag for the key and jammed it into the lock. "Kathleen ..."

"Goodbye, Marcello!" I stepped inside and slammed the door shut, now we'd argued again! And yet everything had just been so nice, it would never work out like this! He just wasn't the right one!

The doorbell rang; I winced. What else did he want? He should go away! "Kathleen!" There was a knock on the door. "Please open up, sweetie! I know you can hear me! I'm sorry. I didn't mean to hurt you. You're absolutely right! I don't want to interfere in your life. C'mon, I want to give you a hug. I'm not going anywhere until we've sorted this out." What was I supposed to do now? I opened the door energetically and his eyes lit up. "Babe, I'm sorry."

"I don't want to keep arguing with you!" I crossed my arms.

"Me neither," he nodded, stepped close to me and took me tenderly in his arms. "I love you, Kathleen," he whispered in my ear.

"You should take me seriously," I mumbled.

"I do. I honor you, very much so."

Now I wrapped my arms around him too. "Oh Marcello, why is it so complicated with us?"

"It's not." He picked me up in his arms again.

"No, you're not supposed to carry me!" I protested, but he carried me over the threshold.

"Where's your bedroom?"

"On the second floor, but I don't want you to carry me."

"I'm strong." He climbed the stairs. "And now?"

"To the right." He stepped into the room and laid me gently on the bed, sat on the edge of the bed and took off my shoes. "Oh, Marcello. It's not working out between us! We're always arguing!"

"That's okay." He massaged my left foot.

I propped myself up on my elbow to regard him. His face was illuminated by the glow of the half moon falling in the window, he was so beautiful! My stomach tingled, I really liked him! "No, it's not. You shouldn't argue so often, especially not at the beginning," I said anxiously.

"Shh ... lie down, relax." Now he massaged my other foot and I let myself sink back.

"Mmh ... that's nice," I mumbled. "Marcello!" I pulled up abruptly!

Startled, he flinched and let go of my ankle. "What is it?" he asked in alarm.

"I didn't even let Claudia know that I'd already left! She must be desperately in search for me by now!" Where was my bag?

He crawled over to me at the front of the bed and pushed me back into the pillow. "Don't worry. This is a village. She already knows that I've brought you home safely."

"And from where? Has she positioned scouts out here in front of the door?"

"Gregory. He saw us leave. He'll have told her straight away."

Oh, that's right, after sitting arm in arm with him! A blush shot up my face. I was very glad that you couldn't see it in this light.

Marcello was now lying on his side next to me, his head resting on his elbow and tenderly stroking my cheeks. "You're so beautiful," he said softly, I smiled. He really could be so sweet!

"Marcello!" I pushed him off me and sat up, startled.

"What now?" he asked, annoyed.

"The front door! We forgot to close it!"

"No, we didn't, I closed it!"

"But when? You carried me, didn't you?"

"I slammed it shut with my foot, now relax! Everything's okay!"

"Ah, how good," I sighed with relief and he pulled me into his arms.

"Don't be afraid," he whispered.

"I'm not afraid!" I said indignantly.

"Oh, no?" he grinned.

"No!" I said firmly. "What should I be afraid of, you?" I laughed briefly and he regarded me lovingly.

"You're afraid of being close."

"I'm not!" I shook my head uncomprehendingly, what was that all about?

"You're afraid that you'll let someone get close to you and then the person will leave you. You're afraid of the pain and the loss."

Somehow that hit me. "That's normal, everyone is afraid of that! Who wants to be abandoned and hurt? Nobody wants that! Do you?" I didn't look at him. "You're always supposed to be the strong one, the independent one, the tough one! But heartbreak is such a bad feeling. I don't want to have to search and search, be disappointed and hurt. I want to be loved for who I am." Tears welled up in my eyes, what a bummer! He would leave me after this outburst! Right away, just get away quickly!

He took my hand and I glanced at him. Love, understanding and compassion were in his eyes, tears ran down my cheeks. He hugged me tightly. Didn't say anything, just held me securely and stroked my back.

I calmed down. I already knew the single blues, but this time it was different. Instead of feeling totally drained and exhausted, I just felt relieved. Like I'd got rid of something.

He kissed my hair. "My strong lady," he said quietly.

"Why strong? I'm totally weak right now," I sighed dejectedly.

"And that's your strength. You are being yourself. You face your fear, you show your vulnerability. That makes you big and strong. You don't run away from yourself. Only when you can be weak you can truly show inner strength."

"Marcello, you're talking nonsense," I smiled and he kissed my tears away.

"So many people pretend to be strong. Constantly proving something to themselves and others. Fighting and putting up a front to set themselves apart from everyone. But you open yourself up to the world. I love you for that."

"But how can you love me when I'm like this right now?"

He stroked my hair. "You are an emotional and passionate woman - I love you for it!"

"Oh, Marcello, you make everything sound so nice." I stood up. "I need a tissue." I ran into the bathroom and washed my face with cold water. Still feeling emotional, I took a few deep breaths, which helped. And now what? Okay, he had comforted me, a true gentleman, but well, I had cried too. He would probably ask politely in a moment about my condition. Then he'd say it was late, that he had to go and that we'd see each other soon and gladly make a run for it. And tomorrow he'd tell me casually that yes, it had been nice with me, but somehow it didn't quite match. It wasn't me, nothing personal. We just didn't have the same vibes, too different views of life, whatever.

There was a knock on the door. "Kathleen, how are you?" Aha, there he was, as expected.

"Good," I shouted. He had done his duty, now he could go.

"Can I come in?"

"I'll be right there."

"Okay." He moved away.

I sighed and returned to the bedroom, maybe he had already left? But then he got up from the bed, my heart was beating wildly. I was so happy that he had stayed! How stupid of me, as he was about to leave me.

He stepped towards me. "Are you feeling better?" he asked caringly.

"Yes, thanks for comforting me."

"Always happy to, my sweetie." He took me in his arms.

I enjoyed his closeness but wanted to brace myself for what was about to come, so I detached myself from him and sat down on the bed. "I'm going to sleep then."

He nodded. "Do you want me to stay?"

"Don't worry, I can sleep alone." I laughed and it sounded wrong.

"I know that. But I'd like to stay with you, if you like?" He smiled invitingly at me and I hesitated. "Don't worry!" he said quickly. "I'd sleep on the floor! If you don't want me in your room, I can sleep outside in the hallway if you wish?"

"I don't know if Claudia would like that."

"Kathleen." He sat down next to me on the edge of the bed, took my hands in his and gazed deep into my eyes. "I know you've been hurt a lot in your life. But I'm not like the other men. And I also know the feeling of pain and loss. I won't hurt you. You can trust me," he added gently. "What do you want, Kathleen?"

"That you stay here with me," I whispered.

"Okay. I'd love to do that." He kissed me. "Would you like me to help you undress?" he added cheekily.

I playfully slapped him on the chest. "Marcello! Behave yourself!" I laughed, he would stay! He didn't leave, he stayed! I was so happy and relieved!

"It was worth a try," he grinned. "Do you want me to sleep outside?"

"I'm sorry, but I don't think Claudia has a second guest bed."

"I like sleeping on the floor! I always sleep there!"

"At your house too?" He nodded. "You do have a home, don't you? I mean, you live in a house, in a room, or do you sleep in the woods?"

He laughed with amusement. "Of course, I have a home! If you like I can show you tomorrow."

"Okay!" I was already curious about that! "Would you rather sleep in the forest every night than in the house?" I was interested now. I had to think about what Benjamin had said about independence and freedom.

"Hm ... I don't know, maybe? I slept in the forest with my father a few times when we went on trips. That was incredible! Lying under the stars and falling asleep and waking up to the sounds of the woods. And then to smell like it. Fresh and at one with nature! And to jump straight into the stream."

"It must be really cold to bathe there, isn't it?"

He laughed again. "Not for us. I do it all the time. My father was a tiger too, as I told you. And when the two of us were out and about, the forest was ours." He fell silent.

"You must miss him a lot, don't you?"

He shrugged his shoulders and glanced to the side. I stroked his back, he stood up abruptly. "Good, then get yourself ready in peace. I'll wait for you outside." He left the room and closed the door, I switched on the bedside lamp. And who was afraid of being close now, Marcello?

I changed my clothes and got ready in the bathroom, lay down in bed and covered myself up. "Come in, Marcello!"

The door opened, he entered, sat down next to me and stroked my face. He leaned down towards me, our mouths met and we kissed for an eternity. Then he cuddled up to me and stroked my cheeks in love.

"I wonder what time it is? And when Claudia will be back," I said into the pleasant silence.

"She's already here."

"What? When?"

"A while ago."

"Do you think she heard us?" That would make me feel really uncomfortable. After all, I was a guest in her house and I couldn't just have an unannounced male visitor.

"No idea. She's long asleep by now."

"But what should we say to her tomorrow when she sees you?"

"I can leave early?"

"But I don't want to lie to her, she's my friend!"

"Well then, I'll have breakfast with you!" he grinned.

At first, I didn't understand the joke, then I remembered that he was a tiger. "Yeah, of course!" I grinned back.

"As you can see, there are advantages to having a tiger friend. You don't need to be afraid that I'll snatch a bite of someone's food."

"In your case, I would use the word devour."

"Devour? Like that?" He nibbled tenderly on my ear and I giggled in amusement.

"Yes, because with animals you use devour, for humans you use eat," I explained.

"But I'm human right now. And now I'm going to devour you!" He grabbed me and tickled my sides.

"No!" I tried unsuccessfully to slap his hands away. "Stop it!" I laughed; he froze and looked startled. "What is it?"

"Claudia's coming up the stairs!" he whispered.

"What?" I asked in horror, oh no! How embarrassing! Had we woken her up? "But I can't hear anything," I whispered back, listening intently.

"Fooooooo...," he replied, smirking, "...led!"

"Oh, you idiot!" I sniggered and shoved him.

"Ah!" He fell off the bed and we both burst out laughing. "She's definitely awake now!" he remarked.

"But then that's only down to you! Why can't you turn into a little shrew? Then I could always carry you around in my pocket!"

He climbed back onto the bed with me and cuddled me in his arms. "Mmh ... I'd love to be your shrew, then I'd crawl all over you," he sighed longingly.

"Marcello, don't be so naughty!" I giggled.

"I'll show you. I would here ..." He let his fingers play around with my décolleté. "And then there ..." They crawled under the comforter.

"Get away!" I slapped his hand and pushed it back out from under the covers.

"I just wanted to give you a theoretical explanation of the little shrew's path," he smiled at me extremely innocently.

"I see, theoretically, yes. And what would be practical then?"

"So practically ..." He tried to cheat his hand under the covers again.

"No, stop! I don't want to know!" Laughing, I successfully batted him away this time.

"I can't leave your question unanswered!"

"That's absolutely okay!"

"Not at all! I'm totally in favor of women becoming just as smart as us men."

"Becoming just as smart? Rather the opposite! That you'll be as smart as us women one day!" I shoved him indignantly, but this time he was expecting it and didn't fall off the bed.

"You see! Men are smarter! I knew you'd want to throw me down and that's why I was able to stop it!" he grinned victoriously and I tickled him. "No," he laughed, overwhelmed. "Stop it! Okay, you've won! Women are smarter!" I pushed him again and he fell off the bed, defenseless.

"Ah, that's nice, space at last!" I stretched out with pleasure, then waited. But I neither heard nor saw anything from him, had I hurt him? I carefully peeked over the edge of the bed.

He was lolling delightfully on the floor. "Ah!" He looked at me. "Alone at last and lots of space here! I'm going to sleep now. Good night!" He lay down on his side and snored.

I grinned. "I hope you're not really a snorer. Because then I'd hit you with my pillow at night!"

He turned back to me and beamed. "Another advantage of being a tiger! Tigers don't snore!"

"Are you sure?"

"Have you ever seen snoring tigers?"

"I don't know. And just because I haven't seen them doesn't mean they don't exist!"

"I certainly don't snore! And my father didn't either!"

"I bet Gregory also doesn't, even though he's human."

He glanced up at me. "Okay, you win. I'll go and you can see him right now."

I knew he was joking and yet there was a spark of seriousness in there too. "No," I therefore said, "since you don't snore, you can stay."

He turned away from me and rested his head on his elbow. There was tension in the air.

... To be continued ...

When is the sequel coming?

As soon as the release date is set, it will be announced on the website and social media channels. So, follow me for specials such as livestreams, bonus stories and other extras.

 www.schwarzertiger.com

Have fun with the book quiz! Here are the answers from Volume 1 Arrival, 10 points for each correct answer!

TRUE/FALSE
1. Ollie beats Wil at cards.
Wrong, Wil beats Ollie at cards.
2. Claudia's aunt is called Marie.
Wrong, her name is Aunt Marchie.
3. When Kathleen is at the Father's, everyone at the table orders the house menu.
Wrong, Gregory takes an omelet.
4. Kathleen wears mining boots in the tunnel.
Wrong, she is wearing her own shoes.

QUIZ QUESTIONS
5. What is the name of the section in which Marcello worked?
Section B.
6 Which initial is embroidered on Marcello's handkerchief?
"G"
7. What is the name of the barmaid at the Father's?
Moni.
8. What is the name of the bar where Paula invites Kathleen for a cocktail?
Bananis.

 BOOK QUIZ Volume 2 Marcello

Have fun with the book quiz! The answers will appear in the next volume. Each correct answer is worth 10 points!   Achieved: (/80)

TRUE/FALSE
(Add the correct answer if wrong)

1. Benjamin plays the guitar.

2. Gregory's mother wears reading glasses.

QUIZ QUESTIONS

3. What is Gregory's father's profession and what is he putting right and who told him about it?

4. What does Benjamin look like?

5. What color are Gregory's eyes and hair and who has exactly the same eye and hair color?

6. What does Marcello look like?

7. Who sits to Kathleen's left and right in the outdoor movie theater?

8. Which animal do Marcello and Kathleen see on their first walk?

BOOK JOURNAL

Title: Volume 2 Marcello, Book 1 Coming Home,
Series: Black Tiger, Author: TWINS,
Genre: Fantasy love story, Published 2024
o Print book   o E-book
Started on: Finished on:
 O O O O O O Evaluation:

That's the point:

What I liked:

What I didn't like:

BOOK JOURNAL

What surprised me:

What will happen next:

Favorite quotes:

Own notes:

Space for your own notes: